Just **please** don't turn the page.

What the HECK?!

You turned the page.
Did you hear me OKAY?

I'll put it down to a simple misunderstanding but
I'll say it once more...
very clearly...

FOR GEORGE

Oh! You opened the book.
I assume that was an accident?
No problem, accidents happen.
I'm not even angry.

PLEASE DON'T TURN THE PAGE.

What are you doing?

I just told you not to turn it.
You definitely heard me.

Look, I was very reasonable
when you opened the book,
but this is **too** much.

Whatever you do,
please DON'T
turn the page.

I'm telling you as a friend
that you definitely don't want to
see what's on the next page.
A young boy saw it once and his hair
turned white with fear.

Whatever you do, **please don't**
turn the page.

Okay, okay... I lied about the
boy's hair turning white.

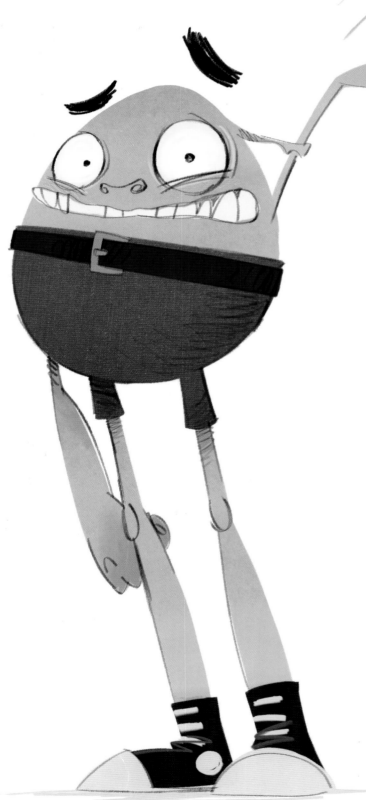

I'm sorry I lied, BUT
you don't understand.
You must stop what
you're doing.

Honest to Charlie,
if you turn the page
I'll **NEVER** speak to you again.
NEVER **EVER!**

Pleeeeaase don't turn the page.

Hmph ...

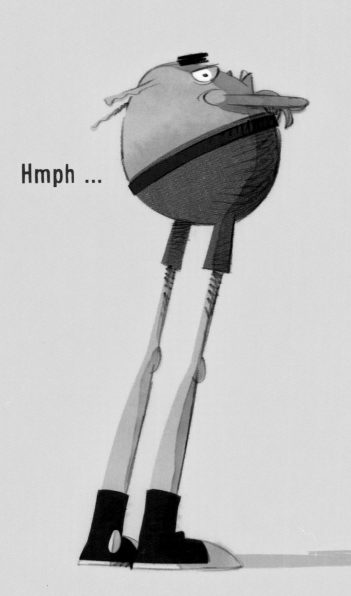

WOW!
Okay, I warned you.
Now I'm calling
your parents.

MUM!! DAD!! Your child keeps turning the page and MUST BE PUNISHED!

Send them to their room!

NO DINNER for a week.

CONFISCATE all books, including this one.

HA! See how you go turning the pages now.

Oh good grief, you cannot be stopped.

Please, PLEASE don't turn another page.

See, I'm crying now. I'm begging. It's serious. If you get to the end of this book I'm done for.

I'll do anything.
You want gold?
I'll get you gold.
You want a flying car?
I'll make one for you.

Just **please don't**
turn the page.

Right... seems like you
can't be reasoned with.

So go ahead,
turn the next page.

That's actually what I
want you to do.

Seriously,
turn it.

NOOOOOO!!!

I was trying to trick you, but it didn't work. You mustn't turn the last page... something awful will happen.

You see, I once met a terrible witch who told me that if anyone made it to the last page of this book she'd turn me into something so hideously, disgustingly and tremendously awful...

So PLEASE, PLEASE don't turn the page.

Thanks a lot.